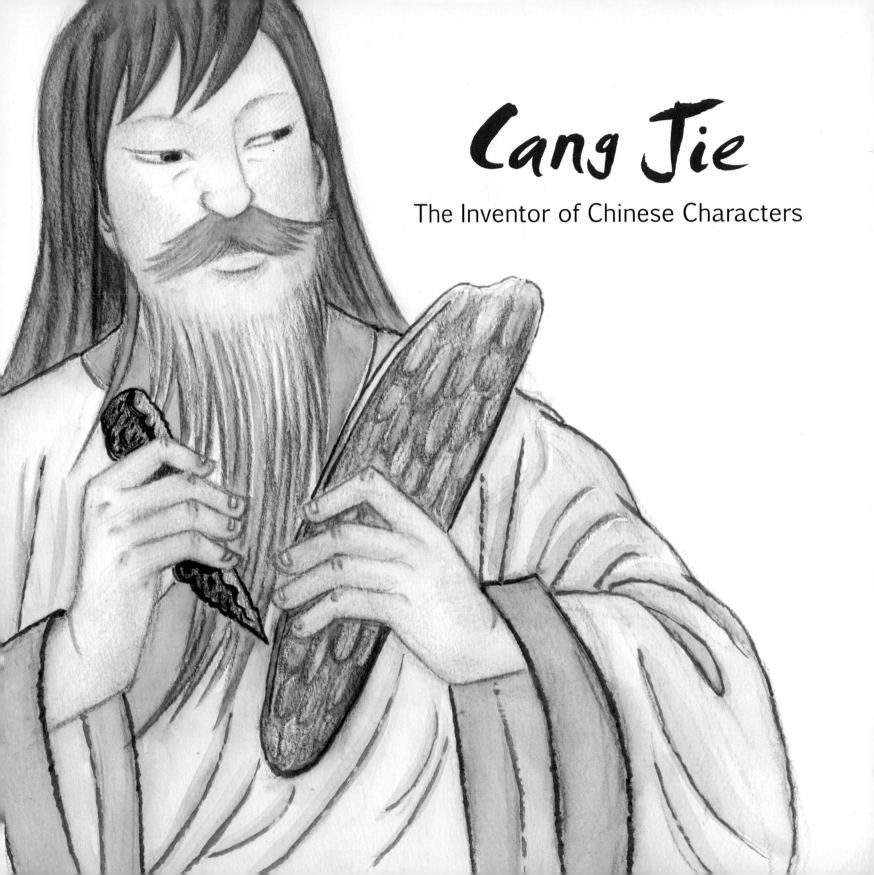

Cang Jie

The Inventor of Chinese Characters

Story and Illustrations: Li Jian
Translation: Yijin Wert

Editors: Yang Xiaohe, Anna Nguyen
Editorial Director: Zhang Yicong

ISBN: 978-1-60220-994-7

Address any comments about *Cang Jie —The Inventor of Chinese Characters* to:

Better Link Press
99 Park Ave
New York, NY 10016
USA

or

Shanghai Press and Publishing Development Co., Ltd.
Floor 5, 390 Fuzhou Road, Shanghai, China (200001)
Email: sppdbook@163.com

Printed in China by Shanghai Donnelley Printing Co., Ltd.

3   5   7   9   10   8   6   4   2

仓颉 Cang Jie

The Inventor of Chinese Characters

by Li Jian

Translated by Yijin Wert

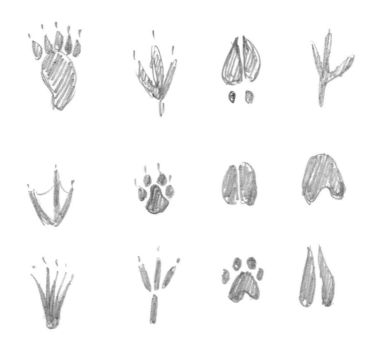

Better Link Press

About 6,000 years ago, the Yellow Emperor became the leader of the tribal alliance of the central region of China.

Cang Jie was the official historian of Yellow Emperor, he kept a record of all the things in the alliance.

约6000年前的中国中原地区，黄帝被拥戴为部落联盟的领袖。
仓颉是黄帝的史官，负责记录联盟中的大小事项。

one two three four five

six seven eight nine ten

At that time, the Chinese characters were not invented yet. Neither was paper or pen. Little stones were used to keep records of events. However, as the number of events increased, it became too difficult to keep the stones organized which made the records incorrect.

那时，汉字还没有发明，更没有纸和笔，人们用堆石块的方法记录事情。但是事情多了，石堆乱了，记录就不准确了。

After this, the knotted method was created. But as the number of events increased, this system created inaccuracies as well.

于是，人们又发明了在绳子上打结的方法来记事。但是事情越来越多，结绳的方法又不能准确记录事情了。

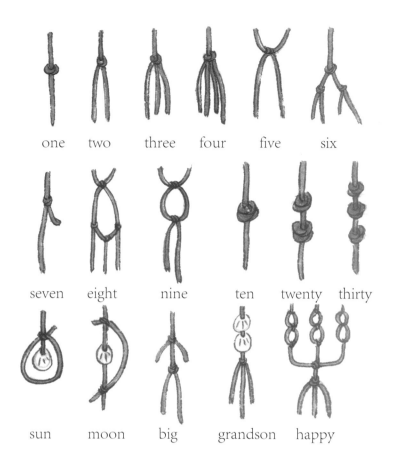

one two three four five six

seven eight nine ten twenty thirty

sun moon big grandson happy

Then Cang Jie created a new method by weaving small objects into the knots to increase the accuracy. He was pleased with the improvement.

这时，仓颉有了一个新发明。他把一些小物件系到绳结里，增加了结绳记事的准确性。他为这一进步而高兴。

One year later, the Yellow Emperor had a meeting scheduled with Chiyou, the leader of another tribal alliance, to discuss the border issues between the two regions. However the Yellow Emperor missed the appointment because Cang Jie made a mistake with his new recording system. When the Yellow Emperor arrived at the meeting point, Chiyou had left.

一年后，黄帝约定和另一个部落联盟的领袖蚩尤商议边界的问题。没想到仓颉新的记事方法出了错，皇帝错过了约期。当黄帝到达约定地点时，蚩尤已经离开了。

Cang Jie was very embarrassed about his mistake, but the Yellow Emperor did not blame him. Instead he encouraged Cang Jie to find an accurate method for recording.

仓颉很羞愧。但黄帝没有责怪仓颉，反而鼓励他找到一种准确的记事方法。

Cang Jie vowed he wouldn't stop working
until he achieved this goal. He visited many
scholars for their insights, but still he could not
find an answer.

仓颉发誓一定要做成这件事。他走遍各
地寻访智者，却毫无结果。

One day, Cang Jie saw a hunter searching for something in the road. He was curious and asked him what he was looking for. The hunter told him that he was chasing after a wild pig by following its tracks. The pig's tracks left in the ground would be able to tell him where it ran off to.

　　一天，仓颉在路上看到一个猎人好似在寻找什么。他很好奇，就上前问他在找什么。猎人说，他正在追捕野猪，所以在找野猪的脚印。野猪留在地上的脚印能告诉他野猪逃向哪里了。

Cang Jie could not recognize the pig's tracks as there were many tracks left by different animals.

The hunter told Cang Jie, "Every animal has its own unique track. I can recognize them very easily." After he said this, the hunter continued to chase down the wild pig.

地上有好多种动物的脚印，仓颉分辨不出野猪的脚印。

猎人告诉仓颉："每种动物都有特别的脚印，我一眼就能看出来。"说完，他就追赶野猪去了。

The hunter's words became an inspiration for Cang Jie. He thought if every object could be sketched with a vivid symbol to depict its main feature, then people could recognize it easily. This would be a very unique recording method.

猎人的话给了仓颉灵感。他想如果每一个物件能够用一个生动的符号来表达其特征，让人们一眼就能认出来，这不就是独一无二的记录方法嘛！

山
mountain

木
wood

水
water

Cang Jie immediately started working on creating the symbol-based writing system. He carefully observed as much as he could throughout the land to create the symbols. The final product was a summary of his findings.

　仓颉立即开始着手创造符号样式的系统。他尽可能多地仔细观察大地创作符号，把发现归在一起就是他的成果。

He created symbols after studying the sky in detail.

他遥望天空创作符号。

云
cloud

日
sun

月
moon

星
star

He created the following symbols after carefully observing human beings and animals.

他观察人类和动物创作符号。

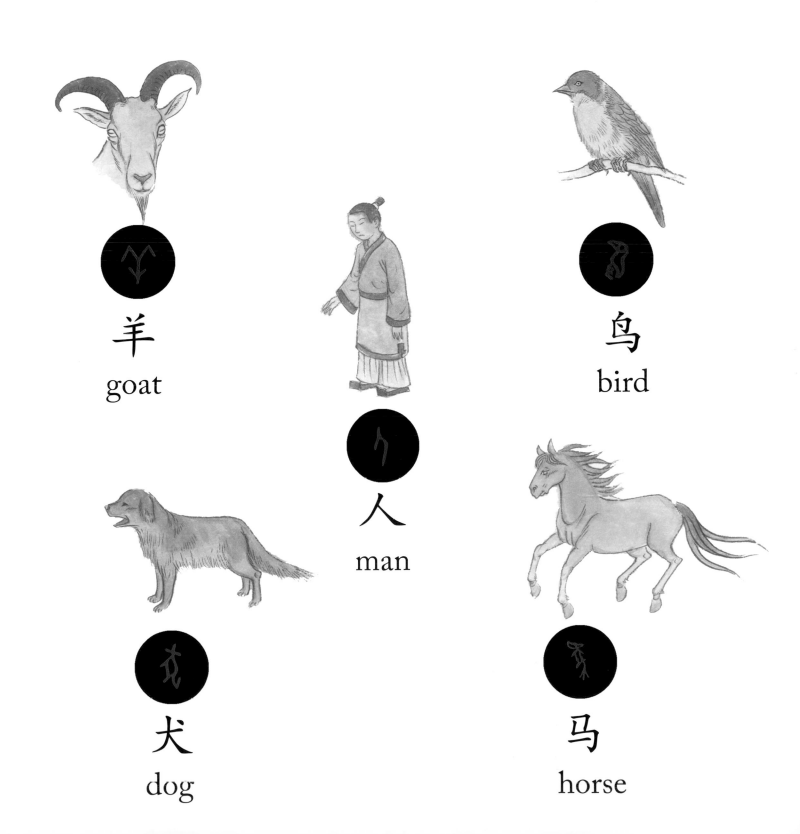

羊
goat

鸟
bird

人
man

犬
dog

马
horse

He created these symbols after categorizing and differentiating objects.

他归纳区分事物的特征创作符号。

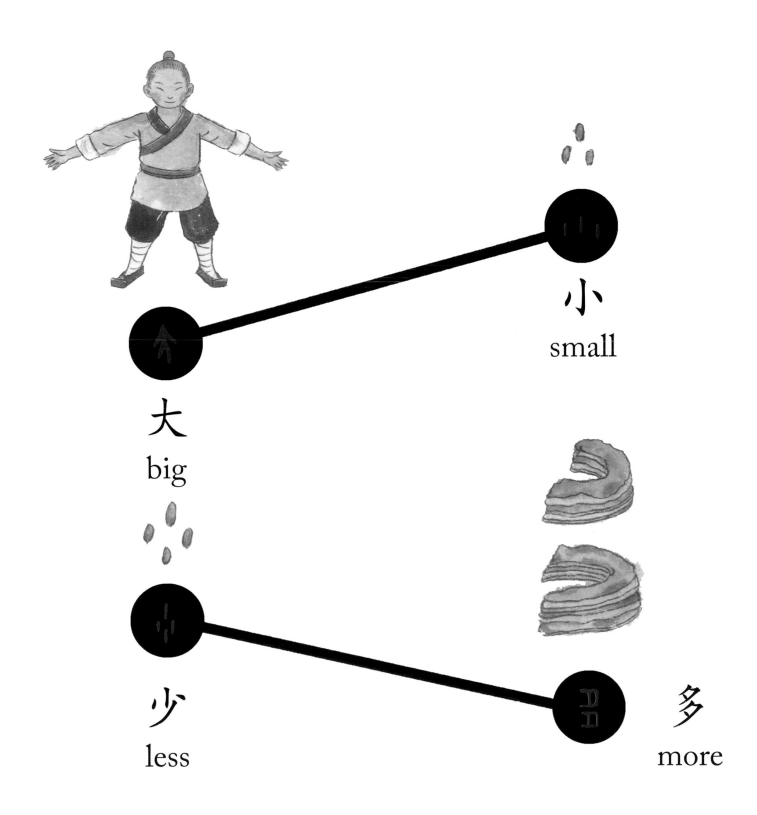

小
small

大
big

少
less

多
more

He created many associated symbols by expanding the existing symbol of 人 (man).

他扩展"人"这一符号，创造出许多新的符号。

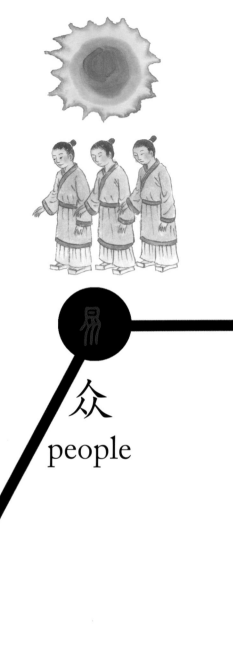

人
man

从
follower

众
people

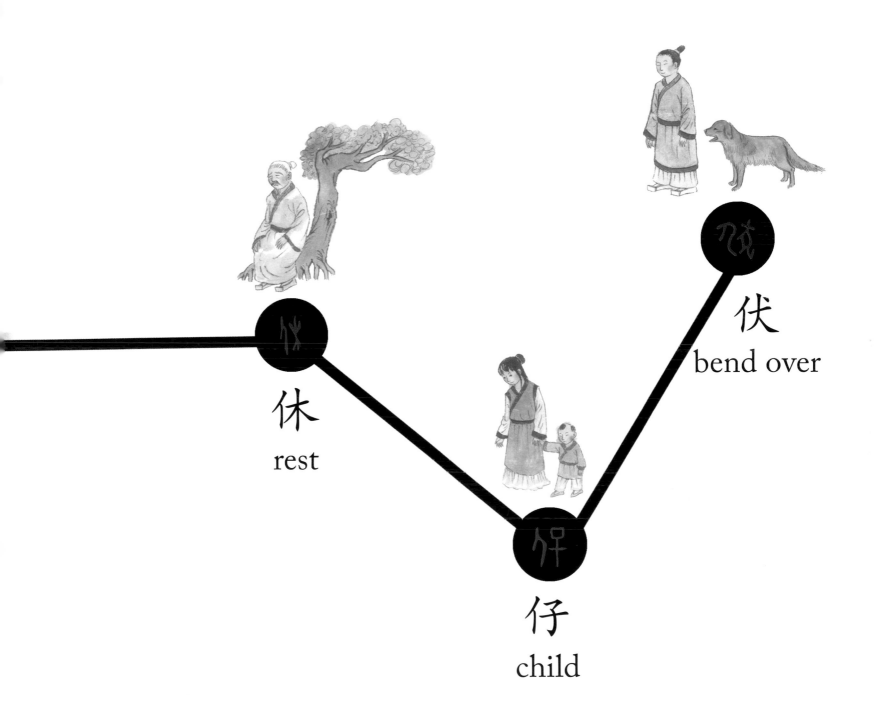

休
rest

仔
child

伏
bend over

He also created many new symbols by combining many existing ones.

他把造好的符号配对组合，又诞生了许多新的符号。

明
bright

夫
husband

吠
bark

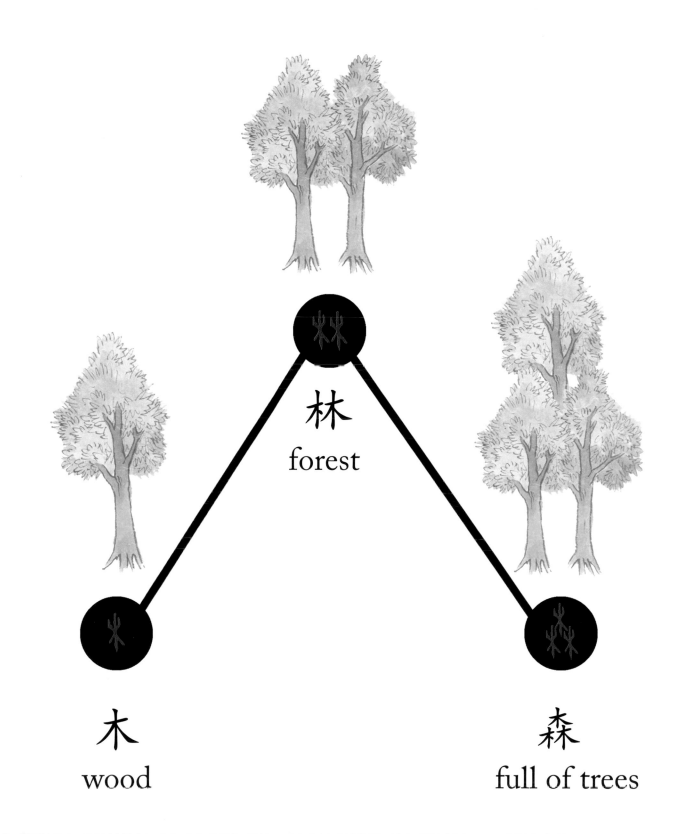

林
forest

木
wood

森
full of trees

The Yellow Emperor called all of Cang Jie's symbols "Chinese Characters," and asked him to teach the writing system to the various tribes.

黄帝把仓颉创造的所有符号命名为"汉字"，要他去各个部落传授字的写法。

Cang Jie also taught people how to draw the new characters and encouraged them to use their creativity. He put a lot of thought into each character to ensure its simplicity and accuracy.

仓颉把造字的方法也传授给了大家，鼓励人们一起来造字。他反复推敲每一个新字，力求最简洁、准确。

On pottery

刻在陶器上

On animal bones

刻在动物骨头上

On bronze

刻在青铜器上

From then on, the Chinese characters were passed down from generation to generation. It went through a gradual process of improvement. It is one of the most ancient writing systems in the world, and it is still widely used in China today.

汉字就这样一代一代传了下去，并不断发展创新。它是世界上最古老的文字之一，今天的中国人还在使用它们。

On paper
写在纸上

On bamboo slips
写在竹简上

On computer
显示在电脑上

On note
写在笔记本上

Cultural Explanation
知识点

Chinese characters have a history dating back over 6,000 years, making it the oldest writing system still being used today.

汉字已有 6000 多年的历史，它是目前世界上仍在使用的最古老的书写系统。

犬 dog

羊 goat

月 moon

日 sun

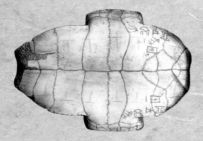

Oracle bone inscriptions were used in China more than 3,000 years ago.

3000 多年前在中国，人们已经使用甲骨文了。

How many Chinese characters are there? *The Grand Chinese Dictionary* contains 56,000 entries, but only 2,500 of them are commonly used in everyday language.

汉字有多少个？《汉语大词典》中有 56000 个左右，其实常用的只有 2500 个。

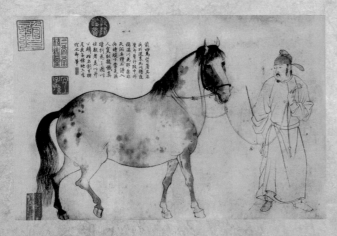

Chinese calligraphy is the art of writing Chinese characters. It can often be seen in Chinese paintings.

中国书法是书写汉字的艺术，并且常常出现在中国画上。

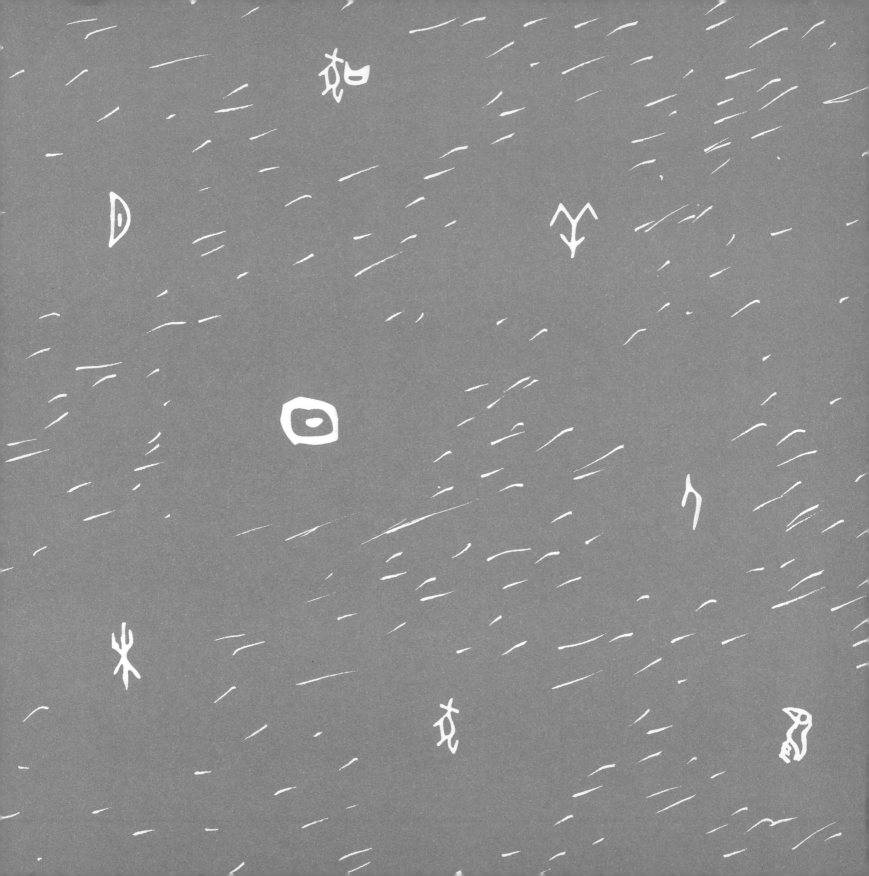